A MONSTER KID
DETECTIVE SQUAD
MYSTERY

BOOK 1

ELSIE FRANKENSTEIN AND THE CASE OF THE DISAPPEARING DOGS

KC CHAMBERT

Castling Books

An Imprint of Castle Bridge Media
Denver, Colorado
Edited by Jason Henderson
Edited & Designed by In Churl Yo
Cover Illustration by Ghost Yo, GraphicsRF.com/Shutterstock

CHAPTER 1

HAVE YOU BEEN TO THE town of Frightsville? It's not as far away as you would think. But some people could search and search and never find it.

And yet, on a certain day, you may be going down the road and suddenly turn the corner, and you're there.

There in the town of Frightsville were all the things that a normal town has—with its public library and its elementary school and middle school and high school. Its hospital and police station and grocery stores.

But then there were things you might not expect: Frightsville's castles, its laboratories, its magic caves, and sometimes, if you looked, its pyramids.

And moving down the sidewalks and playing beneath the trees, alongside humans like you and like me, were monsters.

The monsters lived peacefully among the mortal people and had for years. Or at least they tried. Sometimes the regular people were afraid of the monsters. And all the monsters could do was try, day in and day out, to be good neighbors.

But there was a particular group of monsters who had a hobby that connected with everyone. That was the Monster Kid Detective Squad.

Just a short walk from Frightsville Middle School, in a small forest behind a leafy neighborhood in amongst the trees, near a tree swing and up a rickety ladder, stood the clubhouse of the Monster Kid Detective Squad. The members of the squad were not just monsters, but monster students, and they were dedicated to solving the mysteries that came to them from the children at the school.

When they weren't solving mysteries, they would do what monsters do. They would practice scaring. The Frankenstein twins, Arthur and Elsie, were very good at scaring the other monsters as well as regular people. But the truth was that Arthur hated scaring, because he could look in the eyes of people and see that it made them sad. And that made him sadder himself.

Elsie didn't like scaring people either, because what she really liked, what she liked most of all, was mathematics. And it was difficult enough to find somebody who wanted to talk about that. Especially if they were scared.

Chris and Sherry Dracula, who were separated by a year or two in age, were also not crazy about scaring people. Although the truth was that Chris enjoyed hypnotizing people now and then.

Also there in the clubhouse were Marco Mummy, Rico and Gidge Gillman, who were sea monsters, Henry and Mary Wolf, who were werewolves, Bob Blob, and Mako Seven, who many people thought either came from far beneath the sea, or from an alien world. Although Mako never said which exactly it was, sometimes he seemed to hint that it might be both.

The Monster Kid Detective Squad clubhouse was the perfect place for a young monster to get away. Chris Dracula, who knew a lot about electricity, had managed to bring wires all the way up to the clubhouse so that he and Arthur could play video games. There were a lot of books, and many of them were magical, because Sherry Dracula knew a lot of magic. Sometimes she would take the books off the shelves and lay them on one of the tables. And then she would cast a spell that allowed the characters from the books to get up and walk around before the very eyes of the rest of the squad.

The Monster Kid Detective Squad was called that because they were monsters who solved mysteries. It's not that they wouldn't have let somebody into the squad who wasn't a monster. And all of the children of Frightsville knew that if you had a mystery, the squad was where to go.

CHAPTER 2

"OH, I KNOW WHAT WOULD be really scary," said Elsie. "Imagine that everybody woke up one morning. And all of their furniture started moving around. You know, couches running around, chairs jumping up and down."

"Like the furniture became pets?" Sherry Dracula said. "That's a funny idea. Maybe you could do it."

Her brother Arthur said, "Um… I don't know if it would be scary, though. I think that's something that people would like."

"Maybe you're right," Elsie said.

Just then they heard little bells ringing. Elsie turned around and looked above the door.

There next to a sign that said MONSTERS ARE PEOPLE

TOO hung a little Golden Bell. The bell was attached to a rope that was tied in knots all up and down. The rope went down beside the door, down the wooden ladder, all the way to the bottom of the tree.

The bell was ringing, which meant that somebody was down below and had pulled the rope. Elsie went over and looked down the trap door.

At the bottom of the tree ladder, Benita Garcia, a girl from Elsie's class, was looking up. Benita was holding a piece of paper in her hand.

Elsie recognized the paper at once. It said:

DO YOU HAVE A MYSTERY? IF SO--

CONTACT THE MONSTER KID DETECTIVE SQUAD!

It was a paper that the squad had stapled up all over town.

"Come on up!" Elsie called.

Benita climbed the wooden ladder until she reached the tree house.

"What seems to be the problem?" Chris Dracula asked.

Benita said, "the problem is that my dog is missing!" Her upper lip quivered as she stood there, looking at the monsters.

"Oh no," said Sherry Dracula. "Well, have you asked around?"

"Yes," Benita said, and she began to cry for real, in thick sobs. "But he's not anywhere."

"Where did you last see him?"

"The dog park," Benita said. "We hadn't been there in a couple of weeks. But then we went the day before yesterday, he disappeared. I took my eyes off him for just a moment. And then when I looked back, he was gone.

"And that's not all," Benita went on. "The fact is there have been other dogs to go missing. Something is making the dogs in the dog park disappear."

"Can I see a picture of your dog?" Chris Dracula asked.

Benita reached into her pocket and pulled out a photograph of herself and her dog. "His name is Bluefurr."

Chris stopped for a moment and looked at his sister and the other monsters. "Oh, I see."

Elsie Frankenstein looked over Chris's shoulder. What she saw surprised her.

In Benita's arms was not what she was expecting, which was a fluffy, real living dog. Instead she saw a blue stuffed animal that looked kind of like a beagle dog.

"He's missing," sobbed Benita. "And like I said, he's not the only one."

"Which dog park is it?" Elsie asked.

Benita said, "The Frightsville Dog Park, next to the library."

As Benita was talking, Arthur had already gone to a big chalkboard where there was always a list of mysteries.

And without Elsie actually asking him, he was already writing with a piece of chalk:

BENITA'S MISSING DOG.

This row was under a lot of other rows of mysteries that the squad was working on—some they had solved, and some that were still going.

Next to the name of the mystery was a place for the name of the detective who would take it.

"Well?" Arthur asked. Elsie looked at Benita and then at the chalkboard.

"Yes," she said. "This is my mystery."

CHAPTER 3

ELSIE LET BENITA CLIMB DOWN the tree house ladder first, and then followed after her, and the two of them walked out of the woods. "It's amazing," Benita said. "These woods are right behind the houses. But when you're here, you feel like you could be very far away."

Elsie agreed. She liked it that way. She walked next to Benita, and looked down a little to talk, because Elsie was about a foot taller than the other girl. Partially Elsie was very tall because she was just tall for her age, but she was extra tall because she was a Frankenstein monster, and a special one that would keep growing. Add to that her shock of high hair with its lightning bolt, and she was an imposing figure.

Elsie loved walking in the woods. She enjoyed being with other monsters and not having to worry about people being afraid of her.

But you couldn't stay in the woods all the time. And being able to help people was part of the young monsters' idea in forming the Detective Squad. To make people understand and love monsters more.

They came out of the woods through a wide path that entered the neighborhood between two giant wooden fences. Suddenly they were on the sidewalk of a street which was busy at four o'clock in the afternoon.

"Can you show me the way to the dog park?" Elsie asked. Benita nodded. As they walked down the sidewalk, Elsie saw cars coming and parking in the driveways—parents coming home after work. Several of them hopped out of their cars and ran into their houses, like they were eager to get home and maybe get some supper.

One or two of the parents looked at her and Benita as they walked along. And even though the parents might not have actually walked any faster when they saw her, Elsie felt as though they did.

Elsie could not help but still feel the painful newness of monsters in the town. It had been five years since the monsters that arrived. And truthfully, Elsie had no memory of what had happened— why there were suddenly monsters in the town or where they had come from. She only knew that the monsters were still thought quite strange.

And the people of the town could be nice, but they did walk

a little faster whenever they passed in front of the castles that the monsters had built. Sometimes they looked away from them. But every day Elsie thought it was getting a little bit better.

When they reached the end of the neighborhood, just as they were passing the castle that the Dracula's had put up at the end of lane, Benita pointed across the wide street. "There it is!"

They waited there for the walk sign to turn and Elsie stood beside Benita and looked at the kids and the pets playing in the dog park. There was a big sign over the entrance to the gate that said DOG PARK. When the sign said WALK, Elsie and Benita walked across the street and through the gate into the dog park.

The Frightsville Dog Park was very big, with a pond, hilly fields, and lots of sections of trees. There were grassy areas and areas with no grass at all. Elsie saw places where large dogs played together, and others where smaller dogs played together.

Small, friendly groups of dogs wandered near the gate. There were lots of children and moms and dads busily keeping track of the kids and their pets.

"I've never seen so many dogs," Elsie said. "But where are we going?"

"I'll show you," Benita said. Benita took Elsie's hand and they walked towards a clump of trees near the back fence.

THE CASE OF THE DISAPPEARING DOGS

It was the stuffed animal section of the dog park. Elsie could tell it was a special sort of area all to its own, separated by a slight hill, with another small pond. Everything was fairly quiet. There were a few kids playing by themselves and with one another, but most of them held a stuffed animal.

"Hi," Elsie said, waving. Several of the kids who were about Elsie's age waved back. She knew some of them from school, although no one who is in her own class.

There were a couple of other monsters that she saw.

Theodore Gillman, who was another one of the fish people, was sitting in the middle of the pond, and he waved. He had a stuffed animal as well—in his case, a floating dolphin stuffed with air.

There was also a woman named Amanda pushing a baby carriage. Amanda wore a purple dress and high striped stockings, and a felt hat that was folded over. Amanda was a witch—not the kind of witch that had been around before the monsters showed up, but the kind they had after, who had real powers. But like most of the witches Elsie knew, she was very sweet. In the carriage was Amanda's baby, who waved his plump arms at Elsie. The baby had a handful of golden curls and seemed to be reaching with his arms toward all the stuffed animals.

"Yes, you love looking at them, don't you?" Amanda said to the baby.

"What a beautiful baby," Elsie said.

"Thank you!" Amanda said. "His name is Carl."

"Hello Carl," Elsie said.

Elsie turned back to Benita. "So tell me what happened."

"Well, I was playing here," Benita said, pointing at a section of the grass near an enormous tree where another boy was holding a stuffed horse. "I had my blue dog," Benita continued. "And then when I was pretending to play tag with it, I covered my eyes. And I turned around several times. But then when I opened my eyes, it was gone."

"When was this again?" asked Elsie.

"Two days ago," Benita answered, and she looked down sadly. "I've come back the last two days, looking, and I haven't seen it."

"Has anybody else seen the blue stuffed dog?" Elsie asked, looking around at the other kids. They all looked up but shook their heads.

Amanda looked up from giving Carl a piece of carrot and said, "Dear, I heard that it was missing and I'm very sorry. That's super sad."

Just then, a little boy who was sitting nearby gasped. "My dog!" he shouted. "It's gone!"

"When?" Elsie asked.

"Just now! I went to get a drink of water. When I came back, it was gone. Oh, what are we going to do?"

"You see?" Benita said. "Stuffed dogs are disappearing."

CHAPTER 4

THE BOY WAS SPINNING AROUND as though he hoped he could look in every direction at once. Elsie got in front of him. "Tell me more," she said. "Tell me about the dog."

The boy was starting to sniff, but he was a little scared of Elsie. "You're a monster."

"Yes, there are a lot of monsters now."

"Okay, it's..." he got his thoughts together. "It's a little tan stuffed dog. I went to get a drink and then he was gone."

The baby cooed loudly as a cat passed by.

Elsie looked around at the stuffed dog corner of the dog park with its big tree and all the children playing. She went over to the pond, letting some of the regular dogs sniff at her and move on.

Was it possible someone was throwing the stuffed dogs in the pond? But if so, she would have seen this tan one that had just been lost floating.

So many dogs wandered around, yipping and playing. Some of them gathered in threes and twos, and some of them and wandered lonely on the hill.

And then she saw the orange cat that the baby had laughed at. It was stalking behind a little girl with a tallow stuffed dog. And as soon as the girl set the dog down, the cat pounced.

The cat picked up the yellow dog and held it by the back of its neck.

Elsie touched Benita's arm. "That's it," she said.

As the cat began to run, Elsie ran after it. "I've got you now!" she cried.

CHAPTER 5

ELSIE AND BENITA CHASED AFTER the orange cat with the yellow dog in its mouth. The cat was fast. It ran, holding the stuffed animal firmly by the scruff of the neck, as it stretched its legs and darted around the pond.

The cat ran to a long, bending tree and up its branches.

Elsie had the legs of a Frankenstein Monster and could jump like no normal girl could, and she made huge strides, leaping up even with the cat in the tree.

The cat looked at her—Elsie thought the cat had a merry twinkle in its eyes—and leapt out of the tree, moving on.

The cat darted right past Benita, who reached down, nearly catching the stuffed animal in the cat's mouth, but it slipped through.

Now it was really moving, right over a little hill at the edge of the park, until it reached a wooden fence. Elsie and Benita were close behind as the cat shot through the hole.

Elsie looked at Benita and asked, "Do you want to go over with me?"

Benita nodded and Elsie wrapped her powerful arm around Benita and jumped, leaping over the wood and landing on the other side.

The grass on the other side was tall, but there was a rocky path, and Elsie and Benita ran along it.

Finally they reached a clearing just about big enough for the two girls—and the cat, and the stuffed animal.

The orange cat was playing with the stuffed dog, rolling around with it, putting it down and pretending to stalk it.

"Bad kitty," Elsie said. She fished in her pocket for something to give the cat as a sort of trade, but she had nothing.

"Do you have anything we can trade?" she asked Benita.

Benita reached in her pocket and came up with a small, blue, buttoned jacket. "I have this. It's from one of my dolls. But I don't know." She looked around. "Wait!"

Benita gathered some grass and stuffed it in the little jacket to make it as much like a doll as she could and offered it to the cat.

Then Elsie moved lightning-quick to take the stuffed dog.

The cat gladly accepted the trade. The little stuffed jacket was almost like a mouse, and when Benita and Elsie left the cat, it was stalking the new "doll."

"But the others… aren't there," Benita said.

"I know," Elsie said. "I think the cat is a culprit—but not the main culprit."

The girls carried the stuffed dog back over the fence to the park and returned it to the little girl who had lost it.

But there were so many others still missing.

Suddenly she heard a boy shout, "Go away. GO AWAY!"

CHAPTER 6

BENITA AND ELSIE TURNED TO see the shouting boy. He was about Benita's height, with brown hair and glasses. He was yelling at a dog on the hill that was gray with black spots.

"Why are you shouting at that dog?" Elsie asked.

"He keeps coming up to me," the boy said. "But I don't know him. He won't leave me alone."

"I'm Elsie," she said. "And this is Benita." The boy said his name was Terry.

"Well, do you know whose dog that is?" Elsie asked.

"I don't know," Terry said. Elsie turned to the witch. "Do you know?"

The witch was wiping Baby Carl's mouth and said, "No, I have no idea."

The baby was laughing, pointing at the dog.

Then the baby called out "Nana."

"Oh," his mother said, "I'm sorry, I didn't bring a banana. I wish I had, are you still hungry?'

Then she stopped because in fact, there was a banana in her coat pocket. "Well, you magical thing," Amanda said.

"I wish that dog would leave me alone," Terry said. "I want my stuffed dog, Andy. Not that one."

"Yours is missing too," Elsie said in amazement. "Do you have a picture of your stuffed dog?

"I don't," he said. "But I keep coming back hoping he'll turn up. "

"I have a picture," another girl said. "From my birthday party." She held up a picture of her and Terry playing next to a table covered in balloons and party favors. Terry was holding his stuffed dog. It was gray with black spots.

CHAPTER 7

BENITA SLUNG HER HEAD AND began to walk away from the pond towards the entrance to the dog park. Elsie walked alongside her.

"I guess I'm not doing a very good job as a monster detective," Elsie said.

"I'm happy that you're trying." Benita said.

Elsie stopped and folded her arms. "Let's review what we know: The dogs that have been stolen or have gone missing have all been stuffed dogs from the stuffed dog section?"

"Yes," Benita said.

"And we saw that there was a cat who was stealing stuffed dogs."

"Yes," Benita agreed, "But the cat only stole one."

"And it seems impossible that the cat, or even anybody we've seen, could have stolen seven or eight stuffed animals."

"Yes."

They crossed the street and walked to Benita's house. It was a pleasant little blue wooden house with nice steps in front, and they sat there to think.

Benita went inside and got them some lemonades and brought them back out. When she came back, she said, "I don't know if monsters drink lemonade."

Elsie said, "Oh, yes, we do. Or at least many of us do. I do."

While they drank their lemonade, Elsie heard Benita sigh and look out at the sidewalk. "What is it?"

On the sidewalk, a blue-gray dog had come to the front gate and was standing there, wagging its tail, and staring at them.

"Hi puppy," Benita said. "You should go home. Somebody's going to miss you."

The dog just stayed there. Elsie put down her lemonade and said, "Do you know this dog?"

"No," Benita answered. "I don't know whose dog it is. But it comes here a lot. I don't know. It looks at me. It looks so sad."

"Yes, it does," Elsie said. The dog hung for a while at the sidewalk in front of the house. Then after a while the dog seemed to shake its head. It slunk its ears down between its shoulders and wandered back down the hill toward the dog park.

Elsie was thinking. "Do you remember the little boy with the dog that he said wouldn't leave him alone?"

"That was Terry," Benita said.

"Yes." Elsie stood up. She turned around and put the cup of the lemonade on a little table.

Elsie hugged Benita and said, "I'm not giving up. Tomorrow is Saturday. If you're not doing anything, we'll keep investigating."

CHAPTER 8

ELSIE WALKED BACK TO HER own house thinking how sad it was to have to go to bed without having done what she had set out to. She turned onto Van Sloan Street and walked three houses down until she reached the tall, white-brick castle that her father had built: the House of the Frightsville Frankensteins.

Her brother Arthur was in the driveway with a basketball. Her father had set up a tall hoop and they often used it to play one-on-one basketball. It was a way she could spend time with her brother, and a lot of times, a way that they could think about things while moving.

Although Arthur wasn't very tall, he was taller than Elsie, and his extra-strong monster legs let him jump very high. Elsie stopped and watched him dribble ball clumsily and jump, dunking the ball with a perfect swish. Then he would come down and dribble it again.

Elsie zipped up beside Arthur and seized the ball deftly, springing to swish the ball into the net herself.

"You're back," Arthur said. "Did you find Benita's dog?"

Elsie dropped to the ground and dribbled the basketball a few times. "No," she sighed, and she passed the ball to Arthur. "We spent a lot of time at the dog park, though."

"And?" Arthur aimed a shot over Elsie's head. The ball sailed towards the net.

She jumped, catching the ball, and dribbling it again. "And that place is nice enough, though it's strange. There are a lot of stuffed animals that have gone missing."

She shot the ball and this time Arthur caught it, dunking it in himself. "Two points!" he shouted. "GRRRR!"

"Does that even count if you sink the ball after I shot it?"

"Grr- sure, why not?" He passed her the ball and she held it, then dribbled it away towards the enormous front porch, which was lined with columns. She sat down cross-legged on the front steps, not far from a great stone door with a gleaming yellow knocker.

Arthur looked out at the sky. "Sun is going down anyway," he said. He came and sat beside her.

"Benita gave me lemonade," Elsie said. "I really want to help her."

"You will," Arthur said. "You always do."

They heard the scraping, rolling sound of wheels. Outside the iron gate around the castle, Amanda the Witch came into view, rolling baby Carl in his stroller. As she passed, Carl saw her first. He waved a banana at them. Amanda looked from under her huge hat and waved as well, and they waved back.

"Hi, Amanda! Hi, Carl!" Elsie called.

Arthur got up and opened the great stone door, which creaked loudly. Elsie followed him into the foyer, which always made her happy because her mother lined the walls and the grandfather clock and the furniture with vines, plants, and flowers. The fragrance was strong, and she sniffed it deeply.

Elsie laid the basketball down and looked out the door as she shut it. Amanda and Carl had reached the end of the gate and were moving out of sight. Then something caught her eye.

A little blue-gray dog was walking sadly along about twenty feet behind Amanda and the stroller.

"Shut the door," Arthur said. "You'll air condition the whole outside, that's what Mom says."

"I know that dog," she said to her brother, pointing as she held the door open.

"Hm?" Arthur looked.

"It's a sad little dog that came to Benita's house."

"What about those?" Arthur said.

And indeed, behind the dog she'd pointed out, there came a pair of other dogs. Then two more, and two more. Their tails were wagging expectantly as they followed Amanda.

"Huh," Elsie said.

"Are you guys coming inside?" Came the voice of their mother from the other room. Just then, over the smell of flowers, Elsie realized she could smell a stew of cabbage and carrots.

"Just… just a minute," Elsie said. She started walking out.

"Where are you going?"

"It's a… I have a hunch."

"You do not," Arthur said.

Elsie smirked, looking back. "Are you coming?"

Arthur thought for a moment. "Sure."

"It's still my mystery," Elsie said with a smile.

"You're the absolute boss of this one," Arthur said.

They shut the door and crossed the yard and went through the creaky iron gate. A moment later they were on the sidewalk, following the pack of sad little dogs as they walked down Van Sloan Street.

The streetlights burned yellow as the moon rose and the trees began to look creepier, even to Elsie, a monster. Soon the pack followed the stroller as they turned a corner onto another street in their neighborhood, Root Street.

There was a vacant lot at the corner and Arthur whistled as the dogs silently padded ahead of them. Amanda never looked back. "Does she even know those dogs are there?" Arthur whispered.

Elsie shrugged.

After the vacant lot was a very different house from the Frankenstein's—it was long and flat, and seemed to be made of earth and wood, with moss growing all over it. The front door was circular, with several smaller circular windows where yellow candles flickered from inside. Amanda pushed the stroller up the walk and stopped before the circular wooden door.

The dogs all followed into Amanda's yard, spreading out, ten or twelve of them, all small, all their tails wagging. And now Elsie could hear them better as they stopped. Some of them panted and whined sadly.

Elsie and Arthur stayed at the sidewalk, next to a tree, and suddenly she felt the need to hide.

Why were the dogs following the witch? Elsie got behind the tree and yanked her brother behind it too with a powerful jerk that caused him to give out a very un-monster-like yelp. They craned their necks to look out.

The witch seemed to suddenly hear the dogs as she was bending down to touch Carl's cheek, and she looked back. She stood up straight.

Amanda's mouth hung open in what Elsie thought was surprise. She murmured something to Carl that might have been *what do we have here?* She turned the baby carriage around and Carl clapped and cheered the dogs, breaking the quiet of the night.

The witch pushed her hat back, so that even in the dark Elsie could see Amanda's eyes growing magically with white fire. She pursed her lips.

Thunder rolled and Elsie felt the air fizz around her, causing the little hairs to stand up on her arms. Clouds in the sky, blue and yellow with moonlight, began to swirl.

Amanda spread out her arms towards the dogs and said, "Be gone!" Her voice cracked the sky like thunder.

The dogs turned and ran, all of them, and Elsie and Arthur did too. They ran all the way to the corner and turned, and all the way home. The pack of dogs whimpered and ran, too, zooming past them as the two monsters stopped at the castle.

As they went in the gate, Arthur and Elsie watched the dogs run back towards the dog park.

Elsie was breathing hard and still felt the tingle of the air from Amanda's thunderclap voice.

As they opened their door again, Arthur said, "Do you think she saw us?"

"I don't know," Elsie said. "But I have an idea what's going on."

CHAPTER 9

THE NEXT MORNING—SATURDAY MORNING—Elsie and Benita walked back down to the dog park. This time Elsie had a quicker step because she had a hunch, and whenever she had a hunch, she walked faster.

"Hold up!" Benita called as she walked faster to keep up with Elsie. "You walk fast!"

It was morning and they had a whole day in front of them, but Elsie knew it would be very soon that they would solve this strange mystery.

They reached the gate of the dog park and Elsie said, "Stop."

They stood side by side and Elsie swept her hand along the dog park. The children playing, the dogs running.

"There are a few more dogs here than there should be," Elsie said. They walked together around the pond and back to the tree and stuffed animal section.

When they were there, Elsie saw Amanda the witch and her baby, Carl. Carl was laughing as he made a little doll walk around in front of the stroller. He was waving his arms as it twirled.

"He's really good, isn't he?" The witch said.

"Yes. Do you come here all the time?"

"Oh, yes, every day," Amanda said. "We can't have animals in our house because my wife is allergic, but Carl loves to see them."

The baby cooed and winked at Elsie and she winked back.

"Benita," Elsie said. "Would you call your dog?"

"But he's not here," Benita said. "We already looked and looked."

"I know, but—"

"And he's just a stuffed dog," Benita said. "He won't really come if I call him."

Elsie turned around and put her hands-on Benita's shoulders. "I think you should try anyway."

Benita said, "Okay." Not like she really believed it would help. She looked toward the stuffed animals and the big tree. "Bluefurr?"

Nothing happened, and they heard nothing but the barking of the other dogs and the playing of children.

She looked down sadly, and Elsie said, "Give it another try."

She nodded. "Bluefurr?"

"Loudly," Elsie said. "So he hears you!"

She turned toward the pond and the whole park, cupped her hand, and called, "Bluefurr!"

Benita bit her lip, about to cry, and for a moment Elsie was thinking she might cry as well.

And then they heard a bark. From across the pond, way over on the other side near the gate. Elsie knew what she'd see before she looked.

A dog yapped and began to run. It was the little blue-gray dog that had been coming to Benita's house.

It ran around the pond and came running to Benita until it stopped at her feet.

"But this isn't…"

"But I think it is!" Elsie said. She kneeled, petting the blue-gray dog. "Can I see the picture?"

Benita brought out the picture and Elsie looked at it. The spots were the same. The curly tail against its back was the same.

Elsie turned to the boy Terry, who was playing with some other boys and their stuffed dogs. "Terry, what was your dog's name?"

"Andy, it was named Andy," Terry said.

"Could you call him?"

Terry stood up, brushing off his pants because they were covered in grass. "Now?"

"Yes."

"Andy!" Terry cried.

The little yellow dog that Andy had pointed out earlier came from the side of the pond, yipping around Terry's legs.

"Not you!"

"But I think it is," Elsie said again.

Elsie looked at the two dogs and the two children and turned back to Amanda and her baby. "Miss Amanda?"

"Yes?"

"I wonder if Carl might do these children a favor?"

CHAPTER 10

ELSIE WENT OVER AND KNELT by the stroller.

Amanda smiled from beneath her hat. "I wonder," said the witch. "Was that you and your brother that I saw behind the tree in front of my house last night?"

Elsie looked down sheepishly. "Yes," she said. "We were watching all those dogs."

"Well, I certainly can understand that," Amanda said. "It's very strange. They follow us."

"Do they follow you a lot?"

"Almost every evening," Amanda said.

Elsie looked at the dog that had answered to the name Andy. "Well, dogs want to be loved, I guess. I think…" She pursed her lips, wanting to be right and hoping she wasn't completely off base. "I think that Carl likes making things move with his magic, doesn't he?"

"Oh he surely does," said Amanda.

Elsie tickled Carl's plump little chin. "I don't know if you understand me, Carl, but I think you've been looking at these stuffed animals and sometimes you've been turning them into real dogs. Well, not real dogs exactly. But something like real dogs, that move—and bark—and love their owners."

Carl laughed.

"Here, Bluefurr," Elsie said.

Benita brought Bluefurr over and Carl cooed at the dog as Benita petted it.

"But you see," Elsie said, "these children need their pets the way they were. They love them just the way they were, stuffed, plush, ready to carry home."

"Oh, yes," Amanda said. "Oh, I had no idea."

"Can you change them back?" Benita sniffed as she looked at Amanda.

"I don't know if I can," she said sadly. "Carl was the one who did it."

Elsie shrugged. That made sense. She looked at the baby and took the picture of Bluefurr out of her pocket, showing him.

"Back," she said, pointing to the stuffed animal in the picture. And to Bluefurr. And to Andy, the yellow dog. She looked at several other dogs that were sadly strolling and waved her arm, slowly. "Back, Carl. They need to go back."

Baby Carl leaned forward, babbling a bit. He locked eyes with Elsie, and then looked at the picture, grasping for it.

The plump baby's hands closed around the picture and Carl gurgled, babbling something. He wagged his arm at the living dog. Like it was better like this! He seemed to say.

"Please!" Benita and Terry asked.

The baby frowned and then smiled. He babbled, closing his eyes.

There was a flash from nowhere and Elsie blinked. When she could see again, she heard Benita cry, "Oh!"

Benita held in her arms her little blue stuffed dog.

And Terry held his yellow stuffed dog.

Around the stuffed animal section, children ran and gathered up the stuffed animals that lay in the grass, waiting for them.

"I can't believe it," Amanda said.

"Oh that was so good!" Elsie said, petting the baby's head. "Very good. Very, very good."

Benita cried tears of joy as she hugged Bluefurr, the real stuffed

Bluefurr. "Thank you! Thank you!"

Elsie stood up.

"Welllll," Amanda said, "We're going to have to try some lessons on how not to do this again."

Elsie shrugged. "I don't have any idea about that. But he's so kind. He just wanted to see them happy."

Elsie walked Benita back to her house, and Benita and Bluefurr went inside.

CHAPTER 11

THE NEXT DAY, AT THE clubhouse, the Monster Kid Detective Squad did what it always did when they had successfully solved a mystery. They had a party.

Elsie proudly strode to the board and put a big checkmark next to the line marked Benita's Missing Dog.

The monsters drank red punch and welcomed Benita, who joined them with Bluefurr in her arms. Elsie took her place under long strands of little skulls and crossbones next to the punchbowl.

And because someone always had to ask, her brother Arthur called out, "Tell us how you did it!"

"Well," Elsie said. "Normally if there's a missing dog, you'd go where you last saw it. And if that didn't work, you'd do everything you could, putting up signs and posting online. But we didn't have to.

"Bluefurr wasn't the only missing dog. There had been a lot of missing stuffed animals. And for a while, I thought that a cat who liked to play with stuffed animals had taken them. But a cat didn't need to take more than one to have fun.

"But then I saw that there were extra dogs at the park. And some of the children who had lost stuffed animals, like Benita and Terry, had also had real dogs—or what looked like real dogs—following them around. And then the children wouldn't play with them—"

"Then they followed the baby and Amanda the witch," Arthur said.

"Yes," Elsie said. "And then I knew it had to be magic.

"We got lucky that the baby Carl, who was so magical and so tiny, was happy to change the stuffed animals back. He had been doing it without anyone noticing for days. But in the end, he wanted everyone to be happy. And that was all it took." Elsie put her fists on her hips in triumph.

"And here we are!" cried Benita, holding up her stuffed dog.

"Wonderful," Chris Dracula said.

"It just goes to show you," Sherry Dracula said.

"What's that?" Elsie said.

"We can't be changed. We shouldn't be. There are people who

love us just the way we are."

"And we have to be what we are for them, and for us," Elsie agreed.

The Monster Kid Detective Squad toasted their punch to Elsie and to being what they were meant to be.

THE END

If you enjoyed this

MONSTER KID DETECTIVE SQUAD

mystery book, check out the rest of the series!

BOOK 1: ELSIE FRANKENSTEIN AND THE CASE OF THE DISAPPEARING DOGS

BOOK 2: SHERRY DRACULA AND THE CASE OF THE LUNCHROOM PHANTOM

BOOK 3: RICO GILLMAN AND THE CASE OF THE SEE-THROUGH WOMAN

MORE NEW ADVENTURES COMING SOON!

Find us on Amazon.com

or ask for us in your favorite bookstore.

(Thank you for your reviews!)

Castling
Books

Made in the USA
Middletown, DE
17 April 2021